CRISIS

MARS BOUND

TRACY WOLFF

ILLUSTRATED BY PAT KINSELLA

Spellbound

An Imprint of Magic Wagon
abdopublishing.com

FOR OMAR, WHO BRINGS ME ALL THE JOY. —TW

abdopublishing.com

Published by Magic Wagon, a division of ABDO, PO Box 398166, Minneapolis, Minnesota 55439. Copyright © 2017 by Abdo Consulting Group, Inc. International copyrights reserved in all countries. No part of this book may be reproduced in any form without written permission from the publisher. Spellbound™ is a trademark and logo of Magic Wagon.

Printed in the United States of America, North Mankato, Minnesota.
102016
012017

Written by Tracy Wolff
Illustrated by Pat Kinsella
Edited by Tamara L. Britton
Designed by Laura Mitchell

Publisher's Cataloging-in-Publication Data

Names: Wolff, Tracy, author. | Kinsella, Pat, illustrator.
Title: Crisis / by Tracy Wolff ; illustrated by Pat Kinsella.
Description: Minneapolis, MN : Magic Wagon, 2017 | Series: Mars bound ; Book 1
Summary: While heading to Mars, a malfunction kills nearly everyone on board,
    and it's up to Braden Green, Gabriel Lopez and Misty Everest to figure out
    how to get to Mars.
Identifiers: LCCN 2016948525 | ISBN 9781624021978 (lib. bdg.) |
    ISBN 9781624022579 (ebook) | ISBN 9781624022876 (Read-to-me ebook)
Subjects: LCSH: Mars (Planet)--Juvenile fiction. | Survival--Juvenile fiction. |
    Space ships--Juvenile fiction. | Adventure and adventurers--Juvenile fiction.
Classification: DDC [Fic]--dc23
LC record available at http://lccn.loc.gov/2016948525

TABLE OF CONTENTS

ONE

BREAKDOWN

A huge **BANG** rips through

the *Wanderer* as I get up to put away my

tray. The white metal floor of the cafeteria

shimmies beneath my feet.

I grab on to the nearest wall to steady

myself.

It doesn't work. I **BANG**

my head against the cold, hard wall

as I **CRASH** to the floor.

I don't **move** as I try to figure out what's happening. All around me the other kids are running and screaming. They don't get very FAR. Most of them trip and end up on the floor with me. The spaceship *shakes*.

I'm one of the teen officers in charge of passengers. It's my job to take care of them. But when I try to CLIMB back to my feet, I'm too dizzy. The room *spins* around me.

"What's going on, Gabriel?" the *blonde* girl next to me asks.

Her name is Misty Everest. I know her from my other life. The one I had on EARTH before I was ordered to give up everything to CLIMB on this spaceship bound for the first successful colony on MARS.

We were in high school together back in Texas, one of the most **OVERCROWDED** places on the whole overcrowded planet. Selecting teenagers to join the **MARS** colony that was started twenty years ago is supposed to *help* with that.

Suddenly, a loud **SHRIEKING BLASTS** through the ship. I recognize the sound, though I've only heard it once, in practice *drills* the first night we were aboard.

It's the ship's alarm system, **WARNING** us that one of the ship's outer seals has been breached.

When we were assigned to come on

this one-way trip, we weren't happy. But

we never *dreamed*

something like this

could actually happen.

The captain's voice comes over the loudspeaker, CLEAR and *calm*. "Don't be afraid," she says. "We've had a minor malfunction in a non-vital part of the ship. We have **CONTAINED** the breach to outside corridors B and C. Things should settle down quickly."

Her voice CUTS out.

The last of the **SCREAMS** die out as the alarm shuts off. It helps that the ship has stopped its crazy **JERKING**, too.

"It doesn't feel like a malfunction," Misty *whispers*. "It feels like something awful is happening."

TWO

I think she's right. Something feels off. I climb to my feet. I'm still *dizzy*, but it's *easier* to stand now that the ship is back to normal.

I hold out a hand to Misty. She **grabs** on and I **PULL** her to her feet just as another huge **CRASH** slams through the ship.

The lights go out, plunging

the whole room into darkness.

Misty holds TIGHT to my hand.

"What should we do?" she asks. Her

voice is LOW and SCARED.

I don't know. But I'm not going

to just WAIT around

for whatever happens next.

In every room on the spaceship, there are two EMERGENCY boxes. They are filled with oxygen masks, flashlights, blankets, and water.

We're only a few steps from one. I put my FREE hand on the wall and use it to guide myself forward. I go SLOWLY, so I don't TRIP on any tables or people.

All AROUND us, everyone is getting more and more UPSET.

I raise my voice and tell them, "This is Gabriel Lopez. Just stay *calm*. We'll get everything *fixed*. I promise."

They know me and, I think, trust me. Most of them quiet down. A few are too SCARED to listen, though. I focus on getting to the big ORANGE box instead of on their PANIC.

Despite my care, we *TRIP* over a

few people before Misty and I get to the

EMERGENCY kit.

Once we make it I realize I'm not the only

one with this idea.

SOMEONE

has already gotten

there and is

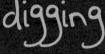

around inside.

He comes up with a **FLASHLIGHT** and turns it on. I realize it's my friend Braden Green, another teen officer on the **WANDERER**.

"Man, I'm glad to see you!" I tell him.

"Me too!" He hands us **FLASHLIGHTS**. "And here, Gabriel, put on an **oxygen** mask. We don't know what's going to happen next."

THREE
DISCOVERY

Once we have what we need, I put two *junior* officers in charge of keeping the people in the cafeteria *calm*. Then we make our way to the **LONG** hallway that runs in a circle around the whole outer part of the ship. *OUTSIDE* the windows, stars *glitter* in the darkness.

"Where are we going?" Misty asks as we **PASS** the teen quarters. Inside, I can hear more LOUD, upset voices.

"To outside corridors B and C," I answer. "I want to see if there's really a **MALFUNCTION** or if something else is going on."

"What else could it be?" she demands, the beam of her flashlight **bouncing** off the metal engine room door.

"An **EXPLOSION**," Braden tells her. "A fire. A collision with **SPACE** junk . . . it could be anything."

a *shortcut* through the empty gym. I nearly **TRIP** on a treadmill.

"She hasn't said anything since that first **ANNOUNCEMENT**."

"What if something happened to her?" Misty asks. "What if the **MALFUNCTION** happened on the bridge?"

"We'll find out soon enough," Braden says as the  goes off again. "It's right down there."

The ship's command center and the hallway leading to it are OFF LIMITS to all but the ship's crew. But right now none of us care. We turn our FLASHLIGHTS off and CREEP down the dark, narrow hallway.

When we get to the bridge, we *peer* in the **BIG** windows that run along the hallway. The only light comes from the **DANGER** sign **FLASHING** on the dozens of computer screens. Nobody is moving.

FOUR

RESPITE

I turn my FLASHLIGHT back on and shine it inside. The crew members are SLUMPED over their desks.

"Are they dead?" Misty GASPS.

We rush inside.

Braden is a teen information TECHNOLOGY officer.

He stops in front of one of the dozens of computer screens and SWIPES across some buttons.

A new screen shows all the *OUTSIDE* corridors **BLINKING** red, not just B and C. "What do we do?" he asks.

"QUICK!

We have to seal the corridors from the inside! If we don't, we'll **leak** all the oxygen." I point to the **WARNING** screen.

"How do we do that?" Braden *swipes* through screen after screen.

"Like this." Misty is in training to become part of the crew. She FLIPS on the **LOUDSPEAKER** at the captain's station. "Evacuate all OUTSIDE corridors," she *YELLS* into the microphone. "They will be SEALED in 10, 9, 8 . . ."

Misty completes the

as she **PULLS** up

the right screen.

Her finger

hovers

above the button.

"If we **WAIT**, we all die," Braden says, pointing to the quickly falling oxygen **LEVELS**.

Misty taps the button. The ship **JERKS**, hard. Seconds later, the alarm stops and oxygen **LEVELS** start to RISE.

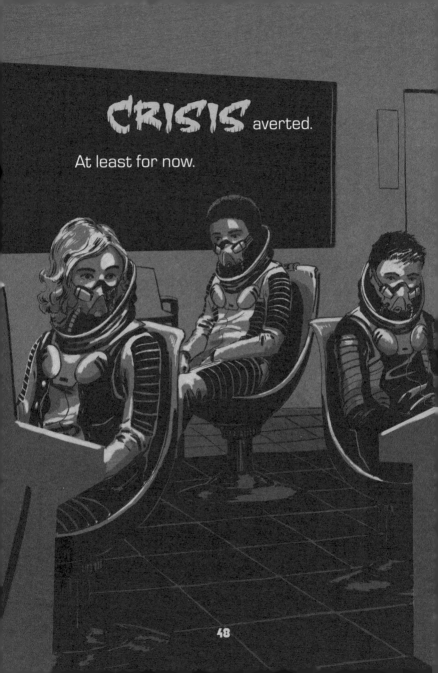